MY LORD, YOUR HUMBLE SERVANT HAS BEEN GUARDING THIS DEAD ELEPHANT FOR YOU.

I EAT ONLY WHAT I HAVE KILLED.

DON'T I KNOW THAT!

I GIFT THIS ELEPHANT TO YOU, MY LOYAL SERVANT.

JUST AS I HAD EXPECTED.

BUT HOW AM I TO GET TO THE FLESH OF THE ELEPHANT?

AS HE WONDERED WHAT TO DO, A TIGER CAME BY.

OH! OH! I SENT OFF ONE FELLOW BY PRETENDING TO BE HUMBLE. HOW SHALL I SEND THIS ONE PACKING?

HE HAS SWORN TO KILL EVERY TIGER HE MEETS IN THIS FOREST.

THANK YOU FOR WARNING ME, DEAR NEPHEW. DON'T TELL HIM YOU SAW ME. I'M OFF.

HA! HA! HA! HO! LOOK AT HIM RUN.

BUT I STILL HAVEN'T GOT TO THE FLESH OF THIS ELEPHANT!

COME ON. BE BOLD AND EAT. I'LL KEEP WATCH AND WARN YOU, IF I SEE HIM COMING.

THE LEOPARD NEEDED NO MORE COAXING. HE BEGAN TO TEAR AWAY AT THE ELEPHANT'S HIDE.

AS SOON AS THE HIDE WAS CUT THROUGH —

HERE COMES THE LION. QUICK! RUN OFF!

THE LEOPARD DID NOT EVEN STOP TO LOOK UP. TURNING ON HIS HEELS, HE RAN FOR HIS LIFE.

THE JACKAL WAS ABOUT TO FEED ON THE FLESH WHEN ANOTHER JACKAL CAME BY.

OH! THIS ONE IS MY EQUAL. I'LL FIGHT HIM OFF.

BARING HIS FANGS HE CHARGED...

...AND CHASED AWAY THE UNWELCOME GUEST.

ALL THIS MEAT! ALL FOR MYSELF! I NEED NOT LOOK FOR FOOD FOR WEEKS.

MORAL: MIGHTY BRAWN IS NO MATCH AGAINST NIMBLE BRAIN.

THE FROG KING AND THE SNAKE

GANGADATTA WAS THE KING OF THE FROGS WHO LIVED IN A WELL. HE COULD NOT GET ALONG WITH SOME OF HIS RELATIVES BECAUSE THEY OFTEN TREATED HIM BADLY.

ONE DAY HE TURNED TO HIS WIFE —

HOW DARE THEY TREAT ME, THEIR KING, IN THIS WAY! I MUST TEACH THEM A LESSON.

TAKE CARE, DEAR HUSBAND, THAT IN TRYING TO HARM THEM YOU DON'T GET US INTO TROUBLE.

BUT, IGNORING HER ADVICE, HE LEAPT FROM PAIL ...

...TO PAIL, UP THE WATER — WHEEL ...

...AND CAME OUT OF THE WELL. JUST THEN HE SAW PRIYADARSHANA, THE SNAKE, SLIDE INTO HIS HOLE

AH! I'LL ASK HIM TO BE MY GUEST AND EAT MY WICKED RELATIVES.

HEY, PRIYA-
DARSHANA!
COME OUT.

THAT'S NO SNAKE CALLING
ME. AND I DON'T HAVE ANY
FRIENDS APART FROM
SNAKES. PERHAPS IT'S
A SNAKE CHARMER!

COME OUT, PRIYADARSHANA.
I AM GANGADATTA, THE
FROG-KING. I WANT TO
MAKE FRIENDS WITH
YOU.

IMPOSSIBLE! CAN
HAY EVER MAKE
FRIENDS WITH
FIRE? WHAT YOU
SAY MAKES NO
SENSE.

I AGREE THAT WE ARE
BORN ENEMIES. NEVERTHE-
LESS, I NEED YOUR HELP.
I WANT YOU TO EAT MY
ENEMIES.

WHO ARE
THESE
ENEMIES?

MY OWN RELATIVES.
THEY LIVE IN THE
SAME WELL AS
I DO.

WHEN GANGADATTA IS NOT AROUND, I SHALL HELP MYSELF TO A FRIENDLY FROG OR TWO AS WELL.

WHEN GANGADATTA CAME TO SEE HIM —

I'VE EATEN ALL YOUR ENEMIES!

GOOD! NOW YOU MAY RETURN TO YOUR HOLE, THE WAY YOU CAME, MY FRIEND.

RETURN TO MY HOLE? YOU CAN'T BE SERIOUS. SOME OTHER SNAKE WOULD HAVE MOVED INTO IT THE VERY DAY I LEFT.

NO, MY FRIEND, I WILL HAVE TO STAY HERE. AND SINCE YOU TOOK ME OUT OF MY HOLE, IT IS YOUR DUTY TO FEED ME.

YOU MUST GIVE ME ONE FROG AT A TIME, FROM YOUR FRIENDS AND YOUR OWN FAMILY. IF YOU DON'T, I'LL EAT YOU ALL UP.

WHAT A FOOL I HAVE BEEN! WHY DID I EVER BRING HIM HERE? NOW I HAVE NO CHOICE BUT TO GIVE HIM A FROG EVERY DAY.

THE SNAKE HOWEVER NOT ONLY ATE THE FROG SENT TO HIM...

...BUT ANOTHER TOO BEHIND THE FROG-KING'S BACK.

ONE DAY, THE EXTRA FROG HE ATE WAS GANGADATTA'S OWN SON; AND GANGADATTA CAUGHT HIM IN THE ACT.

NO! NO! NOT THAT ONE, MY FRIEND. IT'S MY SON!

BUT IT WAS TOO LATE. ALL GANGADATTA'S WAILING COULD NOT BRING HIS SON BACK.

WHAT'S THE USE OF WAILING NOW? WHO IS THERE TO HELP YOU? YOU WANTED TO DESTROY YOUR OWN KIN! YOU'D BETTER ESCAPE FROM HERE OR THINK OF A PLOT TO KILL HIM.

THE DAYS WENT BY. GANGADATTA HAD NO PLAN AND ALL THE FROGS IN THE WELL WERE EATEN. ALL BUT HIMSELF.

DEAR GANGADATTA, I'M HUNGRY. PLEASE FIND ME SOMETHING TO EAT. IT'S YOUR DUTY TO DO SO.

THIS IS MY CHANCE TO ESCAPE.

MY FRIEND, AS LONG AS I'M ALIVE YOU WON'T GO HUNGRY. PERMIT ME TO LEAVE THIS WELL AND I'LL BRING YOU ALL THE FROGS FROM OTHER WELLS.

YOU, WHO HAVE BEEN LIKE A BROTHER TO ME, I'LL NEVER EAT NOW. IF YOU DO AS YOU PROMISE, YOU WILL BE LIKE A FATHER TO ME.

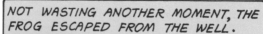

NOT WASTING ANOTHER MOMENT, THE FROG ESCAPED FROM THE WELL.

I'D BETTER FIND MYSELF ANOTHER WELL TO LIVE IN.

MEANWHILE, THE SNAKE WAITED IN VAIN FOR HIS RETURN.

I SHOULD NOT HAVE LET HIM GO.

MANY DAYS LATER, THE OLD SNAKE TURNED TO A LIZARD WHO LIVED IN THE SAME WELL.

MADAM, YOU AND GANGADATTA ARE OLD FRIENDS. PLEASE FIND HIM AND ASK HIM TO RETURN QUICKLY. NEVER MIND IF HE CAN'T GET OTHER FROGS TO COME.

TELL HIM THAT I WILL NOT HURT HIM; THAT I CAN'T LIVE WITHOUT HIM.

AFTER HUNTING IN ALL THE NEIGH-BOURING WELLS, THE LIZARD AT LAST FOUND THE FROG-KING.

DEAR GANGADATTA, WHAT ARE YOU DOING HERE? YOUR FRIEND, PRIYADARSHANA IS ANXIOUSLY AWAITING YOUR RETURN. HE PROMISES NOT TO HARM YOU. SO COME HOME.

A STARVING MAN IS NOT TO BE TRUSTED. I'VE LEARNT MY LESSON. HE WILL NEVER SEE ME AGAIN.

MORAL: DON'T CUT OFF YOUR NOSE TO SPITE YOUR FACE.

THE LION, THE JACKAL AND THE DONKEY

IN A JUNGLE THERE ONCE LIVED A LION WHO HAD A JACKAL FOR A SERVANT. WHENEVER THE LION KILLED AN ANIMAL, HE WOULD FIRST HAVE HIS FILL ...

...AND LEAVE THE REST FOR THE JACKAL.

ONE DAY, THE LION MADE THE MISTAKE OF ATTACKING A FIERCE KING-ELEPHANT.

THE ELEPHANT WOUNDED HIM SO BADLY THAT HE COULD BARELY WALK.

FOR A WEEK, MASTER AND SERVANT STARVED. AT LAST, THE LION HAD AN IDEA.

IF YOU CAN BRING SOME ANIMAL TO ME WHICH I CAN KILL WITHOUT MUCH EFFORT, WE WON'T HAVE TO STARVE.

THE JACKAL SLOWLY ROSE TO HIS FEET AND SET OUT.

THAT'S A FINE DEER BUT TOO FAST FOR MY WOUNDED MASTER.

A FEW HOURS LATER —

AH! A DONKEY! JUST THE ANIMAL, I AM LOOKING FOR!

GOOD DAY UNCLE! WHY DO YOU LOOK SO FEEBLE?

HOW ELSE WOULD I LOOK, DEAR NEPHEW? I HAVE A CRUEL, MISERLY DHOBI FOR A MASTER. I AM OVERWORKED AND UNDERFED.

NOT A HANDFUL OF RICH FODDER HAVE I EATEN IN AGES! ALL THAT I LIVE ON IS THIS DRY GRASS.

THE TERRIFIED DONKEY TOOK ONE LOOK AT THE LION...

...AND RAN FOR HIS LIFE.

A STUPID DONKEY AND YOU COULDN'T KILL HIM! O MASTER, HOW DID YOU DARE ATTACK AN ELEPHANT?

IT'S NOT MY FAULT. I WASN'T READY FOR HIM. I DIDN'T EXPECT YOU TO RETURN SO SOON.

THEN BE READY NOW. I'LL GO AND BRING HIM BACK.

BRING HIM BACK? IMPOSSIBLE! HE SAW ME AND RAN AWAY. YOU'LL HAVE TO BRING SOME OTHER ANIMAL.

I WILL BRING BACK THAT VERY DONKEY. BE READY FOR HIM THIS TIME.

WHEN THE JACKAL WENT BACK TO THE DONKEY—

SO YOU'RE BACK! A FINE SPOT YOU TOOK ME TO! IT'S MY LUCK THAT I ESCAPED FROM THAT HORRIBLE CREATURE!

THE JACKAL LAUGHED.

UNCLE, THAT WAS A LOVESICK SHE-DONKEY. WHEN SHE SAW YOU, SHE SPRANG FORWARD TO WELCOME YOU. BUT YOU WERE SHY AND RAN AWAY.

YOU MUST COME BACK AND MARRY HER. IF YOU DON'T, SHE SAYS SHE'LL STARVE HERSELF TO DEATH.

SHE CAN'T BEAR TO BE SEPARATED FROM YOU. SO HAVE MERCY ON HER AND RETURN. IF YOU DON'T, YOU WILL BE GUILTY OF KILLING A LADY AND KAMADEVA✱ WILL BE ANGRY WITH YOU.

BELIEVING ALL THAT THE JACKAL SAID, THE FOOLISH DONKEY WENT BACK WITH HIM TO THE JUNGLE.

WONDER OF WONDERS! HE HAS BROUGHT HIM BACK! THIS TIME I WON'T FAIL HIM.

WHEN THEY WERE NEAR ENOUGH—

DIDN'T I TELL YOU I WOULD SUCCEED IF I WERE READY? NOW GUARD THIS DONKEY WHILE I GO TO BATHE.

✱ GOD OF LOVE

21

MORAL: DON'T LOSE YOUR HEAD IN THE FACE OF CALAMITIES AND YOU'LL OVER- COME THEM.

THE DHOBI'S* DONKEY

SHUDDHAPATA. THE DHOBI, LOVED HIS DONKEY BUT COULD NOT AFFORD TO FEED IT WELL.

ONE DAY, AS HE WAS RETURNING HOME THROUGH A THICK JUNGLE, THE DONKEY STUMBLED UNDER ITS LOAD, SO WEAK HAD IT BECOME.

MY POOR FEEBLE BEAST! IF ONLY I COULD GIVE YOU BETTER FODDER!

WHAT'S THAT?

OH! A DEAD TIGER! THANK GOD IT WASN'T A LIVE ONE!

* WASHERMAN

23

HE WAS ABOUT TO WALK ON, BUT SUDDENLY STOPPED.

THAT'S IT! I'LL FLAY THIS FELLOW AND TAKE THE SKIN HOME. MY DONKEY WILL NO LONGER LACK FOOD.

YOU WILL SOON BECOME A FEARFUL TIGER, MY GENTLE DONKEY, AND EAT ALL THE MILLET YOU WANT.

THERE! NOW, IN THIS GARB, GO INTO THE MILLET FIELDS AT NIGHT.

THAT NIGHT —

COME. IT'S TIME FOR YOU TO CHANGE.

THE DHOBI THEN LED HIM TO THE MILLET FIELDS.

GO, MY PET, AND EAT TO YOUR HEART'S CONTENT. I'LL COME BACK FOR YOU IN THE MORNING.

AN HOUR LATER, WHEN THE FARMER AND HIS MEN CAME TO MAKE THEIR USUAL ROUNDS—

THERE'S AN ANIMAL IN THE MILLET FIELD!

IT'S A TIGER! RUN!

AND THE DONKEY MUNCHED AWAY UNDISTURBED.

IN THE MORNING, THE DHOBI LED HIM HOME. THIS WENT ON FOR MANY DAYS.

YOU'VE GROWN SO PLUMP, MY DONKEY. IF YOU GROW ANY PLUMPER, YOU WILL NOT BE ABLE TO ENTER YOUR STALL.

ONE NIGHT—

THERE HE IS AGAIN!

WHAT SHALL WE DO? WE'RE HELPLESS.

JUST THEN, THE DONKEY HEARD THE BRAY OF A SHE-DONKEY.

EE-AW !

EE-AW

WE'VE BEEN DUPED. IT'S ONLY A DONKEY IN DISGUISE!

THE ANGRY FARMER AND HIS MEN CHARGED AT THE DONKEY AND BEAT HIM TO DEATH.

IN THE MORNING, THE DHOBI WAS SHOCKED TO SEE HIS DONKEY DEAD.

ALAS, MY FRIEND! HOW DID IT HAPPEN?

MORAL: SILENCE IS GOLDEN.

THE LIONESS AND THE JACKAL CUB

A LIONESS ONCE GAVE BIRTH TO TWO CUBS AND FOR A TIME COULD NOT GO OUT HUNTING.

SO HER HUSBAND WENT OUT...

...AND BROUGHT HOME THE GAME HE KILLED.

ONE DAY, HE COULD NOT FIND AN ANIMAL TO KILL. AS HE WAS RETURNING HOME —

WHAT'S THAT? A JACKAL CUB?

HE RAISED HIS PAW TO STRIKE IT WHEN PITY FOR THE TINY CREATURE OVERCAME HIM.

NO! HE'S JUST A CUB.

27

HOW CAN I KILL HIM?

PICKING THE CUB UP GENTLY WITH HIS TEETH...

...HE TOOK IT HOME ALIVE.

WHAT HAVE YOU BROUGHT TODAY?

I COULDN'T FIND A SINGLE ANIMAL. THEN I SAW THIS CUB. I DIDN'T HAVE THE HEART TO KILL HIM.

BUT YOU MAY KILL AND EAT HIM IF YOU LIKE.

WHEN YOU DIDN'T HAVE THE HEART TO KILL HIM, HOW CAN I?

HE SHALL GROW UP AS MY THIRD SON.

THE THREE CUBS SOON GREW PLUMP AND FRISKY.

28

ONE DAY —

WHO IS THAT INTRUDER? COME, BROTHERS, LET'S GO AND ATTACK HIM.

WAIT, BROTHERS. DON'T! THAT'S AN ELEPHANT. AN ENEMY OF OUR RACE. LET'S RUN AWAY!

RUN AWAY? HA! HA!

WHAT'S SO FUNNY? I'M GOING TO RUN AWAY. LET THEM FOLLOW IF THEY WANT TO.

LATER AT THE DEN —

...AND, MOTHER, IT WAS SO FUNNY! HO! HO! THE WAY HE PUT HIS TAIL BETWEEN HIS LEGS. HA! HA!...

HO! HO... AND RAN FOR HIS LIFE... HA! HA!

YOU ARE FOOLS. I SHOULD HAVE LET THAT ELEPHANT KILL YOU. I WISH I HADN'T WARNED YOU. I...

CALM DOWN, MY SON. LET US GO OUTSIDE. I WANT TO TALK TO YOU.

WHEN THEY WERE ALONE —

YOU MUST NEVER AGAIN SPEAK LIKE THAT TO THEM. THEY ARE YOUR OLDER BROTHERS.

SO WHAT? DO YOU THINK I AM INFERIOR TO THEM IN ANY WAY? WHY DO THEY MAKE FUN OF ME? I'M GOING TO KILL THEM!

THE LIONESS HELD BACK THE SMILE THAT CAME TO HER LIPS.

POOR CUB. I WILL HAVE TO TELL HIM THE TRUTH— BEFORE IT'S TOO LATE.

MY CUB, YOU ARE THE SON OF A JACKAL. I BROUGHT YOU UP BECAUSE YOU WERE HELPLESS.

AS LONG AS MY SONS ARE CUBS, THEY WILL NOT HARM YOU. RUN AWAY AND JOIN YOUR OWN PACK BEFORE THEY KNOW YOU TO BE A JACKAL.

IF YOU DON'T, MY SONS WILL SOONER OR LATER FIGHT YOU AND KILL YOU.

THE POOR JACKAL WAS SO TERRIFIED WHEN HE HEARD THIS, THAT WITHOUT A WORD HE SLUNK AWAY TO FIND HIS OWN PACK.

MORAL: YOU ARE BEST OFF WITH YOUR OWN KIND.

THE STORY OF AMAR CHITRA KATHA

50 YEARS

AMAR CHITRA KATHA

A YEAR-LONG CELEBRATION OF FIVE DECADES OF STORYTELLING

WE PROUDLY PRESENT A SERIALISED RETELLING OF HOW OUR BELOVED FOUNDER, UNCLE PAI, FIRST STARTED AMAR CHITRA KATHA AND TINKLE!

LOOK OUT FOR A ONE-PAGE COMIC IN EVERY ISSUE THIS YEAR!